The Magic Bed

John Burningham

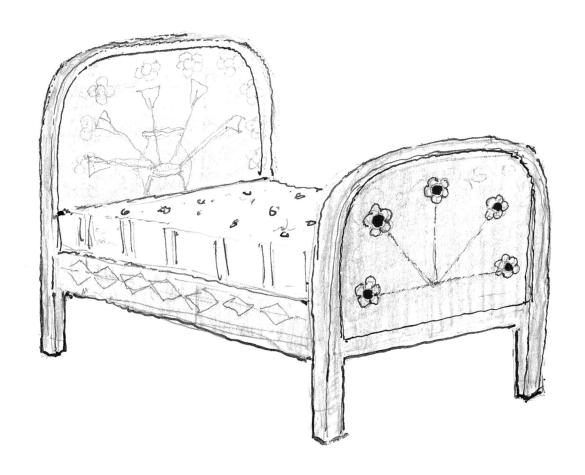

Alfred A. Knopf 🐎 New York

To Harriet

THIS IS A BORZOI BOOK PUBLISHED BY ALFRED A. KNOPF

Text and illustrations copyright © 2003 by John Burningham

All rights reserved under International and Pan-American Copyright
Conventions. Published in the United States by Alfred A. Knopf, an imprint of
Random House Children's Books, a division of Random House, Inc., New York, and
simultaneously in Canada by Random House of Canada Limited, Toronto. Distributed by
Random House, Inc., New York. Originally published in Great Britain in 2003
by Jonathan Cape, a division of Random House UK Limited.

KNOPF, BORZOI BOOKS, and the colophon
are registered trademarks of Random House, Inc.

www.randomhouse.com/kids

Library of Congress Cataloging-in-Publication Data

Burningham, John.
The magic bed / by John Burningham
p.   cm.
Summary: Georgie gets a new bed that takes him on magical adventures.

ISBN 0-375-82423-5 (trade) — ISBN 0-375-92423-X (lib. bdg.)

[1. Beds—Fiction. 2. Magic—Fiction.] I. Title.

PZ7.B936 Mag 2003
[E]—dc21   2002075428

Printed in Malaysia

September 2003

10 9 8 7 6 5 4 3 2 1

"That bed is far too small for you now, Georgie.
Why don't you and Frank go down to the shopping
center to buy a new one?" said Georgie's granny.

On the way to the shopping center, Georgie saw
a shop that sold old furniture.
"Look, Frank," said Georgie. "Maybe they'll
have a bed in there."

They parked the car and went into the shop.

"Do you have a bed that would be right
for this boy?" said Frank.
"Beds . . . beds . . . yes, I do have a little
old bed somewhere," said the man.

After some time, the man found the bed.
"The lady this bed came from
said it was magic," he said.
"And that you could travel in it."

Frank and Georgie bought the bed.
They tied the bed to the top of the car and took it home.

Georgie and Frank cleaned the bed all over.

"Look, Georgie," said Frank, "there's some writing here. It's very faint."

"What does it say?" said Georgie.

"It says: 'In this bed you will travel far.

First say your prayers and then say...'

I can't read the last word. It says M, something, something, something, Y."

"What on earth have you got there?" said Georgie's granny.
"Why did you get that awful old bed? Why didn't you go
to the shopping center and buy a new one?"
"It's a lovely bed," said Georgie, "and it's magic. You can travel in it."

That evening, Georgie got ready for bed early.

He said his prayers and then tried to say the magic word.
He tried: money, matey, mummy, murky, molly, mandy,
milly, messy, minty, mousy...
But nothing happened and Georgie went to sleep.

"How did you get on last night in your magic bed?
Did you go to the moon or up the Amazon?" his granny
asked him at breakfast.

That night, Georgie went to bed early again and tried to guess
the magic word. He must have got it right because suddenly . . .

he was traveling way over the city.

Georgie's bed landed in a field.
Lots of gnomes and fairies
arrived and he read them
a bedtime story.

At breakfast the next day, Georgie
decided not to tell anyone about
where he had been during the night.

That evening, Georgie was off again.
This time he was traveling over the jungle.

Georgie came across a young tiger that was lost.
It had wandered away from its parents and didn't
know how to get back home.

He took the young tiger back to its
mother and father, who were very pleased
that Georgie had found their child.

On one of his journeys, Georgie found
a chest full of treasure in a cave.

But there were some pirates who were very
angry because they thought the treasure was theirs.

They chased Georgie down the beach . . .

. . . and he only just managed to escape.

Some nights, Georgie would go for a swim with the dolphins, which is why his bed was sometimes wet in the mornings.

Another night, Georgie gave a lift to some geese
that were very tired because they had flown a long way.
Then he raced against some witches.

Then came the day that they were off on their holidays.
They waved goodbye to Georgie's granny and set off.

While they were away, Georgie forgot all about his magic bed.

The holiday soon came to an end,
and they all came home.

"There is a lovely present for you, Georgie.
It's in your room," said his granny.

Georgie rushed up to his room and
there in the corner was a brand-new bed.
"What have you done with my magic bed?"
said Georgie.
"Oh, that nasty old bed went down to the
dump today," said Granny.

Georgie raced out of the house, down the steps,
and along the road to the dump.

He just managed to get through the gates as the dump was closing.
There, on top of a dumpster, was Georgie's magic bed.

Georgie climbed up into the dumpster. He jumped onto his bed, said the magic word, and the bed rose quickly into the sky.

Now, if you lie very still in your bed and find *your* magic word, perhaps you could travel far away like Georgie.